BACKGROUND MUSIC

for my grandchildren –
Cameron and Euan,
Izzy and her big sister Hannah

BACKGROUND MUSIC

Cynthia Fuller

*Flambard*Press

First published in Great Britain in 2009 by Flambard Press Ltd
16 Black Swan Court, 69 Westgate Road, Newcastle upon Tyne NE1 1SG
www.flambardpress.co.uk

Typeset by BookType
Cover Design by Gainford Design Associates
Front cover painting: 'Esh Winning' by Tess Spencer
Printed in Great Britain by Cpod, Trowbridge, Wiltshire

A CIP catalogue record for this book is available from the British Library.

ISBN: 978-1-906601-10-2

Flambard Press wishes to thank Arts Council England
for its financial support.

Flambard Press is a member of Inpress

Contents

Family Album

1. *My Mother as Euphrosyne*

I could be looking through the viewfinder.
It is Derwentwater, 1934.
There are three young women paddling.

Three Graces, my mother in the middle,
one arm is round her almost sister-in-law,
the other round her closest friend from school.

There is something sneaky in this stolen
look, when I only knew them sensible
and grown up, never youthful nor playful.

It feels like cheating that I know the rest –
Madge will lose her husband young,
Laura's mother will live on and on

in the corner of her marriage. I can't
unknow it, but can let them linger here,
three Graces to rejoice the heart,
up to their shins in hope and sunshine.

2. Telling Fortunes

Take home a dated record of your weight
and fortune, the sign behind them says,
among the plaques for *Capstan* and *Gold Flake*.
1934 and Europe far away,
I am spying on my parents, hardly
know them, horsing around on holiday,
no lines yet, all their teeth and hair, and happy,
in droopy woollen swimsuits at Whitley Bay.

I can see the printed fortune they took home
was kinder than the one that would evolve.
I'd like to slip – an unborn ghost – between them
to whisper, 'Make the most of all that love.'
I'd nudge my dad towards a different path,
take the habitual fag out of his mouth.

3. Beside the Seaside

As he picks his way across the beach
with that tin tray of drinks he looks carefree,
boyish – as if 28 were younger then.
This holiday's a jaunt up north with pals,
young couples dreaming weddings and bright futures.

This is time out from work, escape from
engines, vans and balancing the books.
Time for a game of cricket on the sand,
days that hold no parting from his girl.

But when he brings the morning papers back
to the cosy guest-house breakfast table,
can he feel the news wash in from Europe,
oil slicks spreading through their summer sea?

*

Did they talk about it in between the jokes
as they walked along the pier, looked out
to sea – Germany rearming, Hitler's
rise? Too young for the last war they lived
in its backwash still – older brothers,
cousins, friends who had not returned.

Or did it all seem safely far away
from the beach, the prom where girls were strolling?
The caption reads 'Our Lads on Holiday'–
Geoff muscular in trunks, Harry with trousers
rolled up over bony knees – both saving
for rings, looking to settle down, as if
a stretch of sea between would be enough
with such a dark storm brewing.

4. *Two Photographs*

I do not recognise them as they squint
into the camera, faces pinched and strained.
Wet woolly bathing costumes do not flatter –
he is pale and thin, she plump, ungainly.
How she would hate that view, so here's another
bright with smiles, washed and dressed in style –
her beret jaunty, his shirt crisp white,
no cigarette for once between his fingers.

In the first snap they are touching, but
the way the sun discomforts them, the way
she shields her belly with an arm suggests
how hard it will be. The second shows what
I could never know – how love transfigured them.
Their faces are soft with it, their eyes brim.

Bruxelles, 1937

She took her English style and school room
French to Bruxelles. It was her father's plan
to put the Channel's breadth between them –
out of sight, he thought, her lover's power would wane.
But the precise italics of his words
spilled love so fierce her heart grew surer still.
Love accompanied her along the boulevards,
stayed close as she taught her solemn pupils,
Etienne and Michel, who caught a touch of it,
eyes bright for her behind their spectacles.
(They wrote to her each New Year, never forgot.)
She brought home fluent French, a bridal veil
of finest Belgian lace. Her father gave
her away to my father – neither giving way.

Hill Crest

They Stand for the Camera, 1921

With the house as backdrop they stand
for the camera, my mother and her family.
It is solid built, detached, suitable

for her father, the college principal.
Its windows gleam, its corners are sharp,
its tiles from Europe flushed with success.

Be-hatted parents – the father
in waistcoat, tie, stiff-collar-formal,
his hand on his wife's shoulder, her smile

uncertain, despite the pretty clothes.
The scholarships are won; behind them
their fathers – post master and clog maker,

the village at the other end of England.
The house measures how far they've come.

It Seemed Like a Game, 1959

It seemed like a game at first, Sunday
expeditions with a picnic in August
heat; two buses and a steep climb to find

the garden shoulder high as if a spell
had made it grow up round the sleeping house.
We slashed at it with scythes, raked and gathered it

in armfuls for wild toppling bonfires.
We uncovered statues flat like corpses,
a pond choked with dirt. Steps and lawns appeared.

We spread our picnic rug in the wilderness,
fatigue turning us heavy and slow, beaten
by nettles and sunburn. The house looked on.

Its cool dim rooms were waiting for us,
as if we could cut through briars, break the spell.

My Mother Wanted To Go Home

As the money slipped away my mother wanted
to go home, to the house on the hill where
friendly ghosts would replace neighbours' gossip.

She bargained for her brothers' shares, expelled
the tenants who'd let in neglect, kept a horse
in the kitchen. She took our family there.

Everything rattled. Poplar roots lifted
the floors, opened cracks, interfered with doors.
There were rats in the plum trees, dead birds
in the chimneys, ceilings bulging with damp.

My father made it his life's work to restore
the house to her, to make it up to her, as if
he could silence the whispers *He isn't*
good enough that waited in every room.

How Must It Have Been

How must it have been for her, going back
to rooms she lived in as a girl, meeting
her young self dressed up for a night out
with the young man who was now downstairs
weighed down with what had not worked out, and silent.

And how did it feel to him – once an unwelcome
suitor in this house, ex-pupil of her father's,
labelled rebel, scholarship potential, lost
to the family firm, now trying to salvage
what he could for her, for them all, from failure.

There was more to bring in the packing cases
than our goods and chattels. I hope they sat late
into the night, weighing each fear together,
a close communion that we never saw.

Roads

The way you think you know is strange now.
Hedges have grown up to block the view.
Street lamps have given way to stars.
The clinking masts of yachts have turned
into the ghostly bells you always feared.

The road going straight ahead has poplars
casting blue shadows like measured intervals.
Sun has baked the surface dry as bone.
What lies beyond the poplars can't be seen.
There is only road, a flat bleached tape.

The hilly road hides in a tunnel of alder.
Arched ribs of trunks close, enclose until
it floats in underwater leaf light.
Any moment small hooves might dainty across.
Who can say whether deer or unicorn.

The road already travelled isn't there.
Put on your shoes again and choose.

Sanctuary

Dumped at the roadside, all her thoughts broken,
mouth no longer her mouth, see her dart
like a creature freed from the headlamps
into the forest's safe dark.

Bare feet are not hurt by the carpet
of pine needles. Moss staunches bleeding.
Moonlight cools bruises. Her blood beat
will settle now, her body cease shaking.

Her heart as it calms knows no harm is meant
in the scuffle of paws, no danger
for her in the rustle of dead leaves.
She is no prey for wild hunters.

She lets low branches whip back, relishes
sharp thorns and nettles, clean pain to wipe out
the marks of soiled fingers, cold earth to
put out her belly's hurt burning.

Her pulse slows, around her a new rhythm,
tuned to the owl's wing brushing the darkness,
the flare of the fox as he catches a scent,
the delicate hesitancy of the deer.

And perhaps she will stay, let the wildness take her,
her scraped arms resting, eyelids closing,
tangled hair a nest for earwigs and woodlice,
bruised mouth a fruit on the forest floor.

Johnson's Pond

Water fathoms deep
even at edges where roots
tripped us, reed stands hid
the bank's lip, we'd slip
in up to our knees.
No one dared the middle
not on the hottest days.
They said a cow drowned there.

Wherever your jar dipped
through soft green scum
it flashed with sticklebacks,
minnows and emerald weed.
Fishing done, we sat in silence,
waiting, watching
the middle of the pond,
so still horseflies settled.

Water was cleaner there
but inky dark. Sky floated,
water boatmen sculled,
dragonflies dipped and shone.
When slow bubbles
disturbed the surface
we did not speculate,
each in our separate fear.

But at night, too hot to sleep,
I thought of the pond
cool and deep, dark creatures
rustling down to drink,
saw myself crossing the field,
small girl in pyjamas
startling quiet cows,
to be the only one there.

In the moonlight
I saw a line and float
bobbing at the pond's centre,
the bulk of a person
hunched waiting,
waiting so long
the willow of his rod-rest
was budding.

Rapunzel

A witch's child, we said,
the mother at the school gate
older than everyone's Nan.

Top juniors, we helped out
in reception, did shoe laces,
buttons, straps, after P.E.

Even her knickers and vest
were knitted: tucking her in
I smelled bread fresh baked,

sun on damp wool, in the layers
of bodice, stockings, petticoat,
blouse and pleated skirt, stitches

plain and purl, ribbed and trimmed
with eyelets and threaded ribbons,
like the clothes worn by our dolls.

She stood four square to be helped,
cheeks' bloom of the best apple,
creamy nape feathered with wisps

strayed from the coronet of plaits.
Her sturdy limbs were just
what a witch would eat.

Imprisoned in a childhood
from another age, I wonder
how she fared later.

I hope she didn't wander
in the wilderness too long,
her sweetness going to waste.

If she kept one jot of the charm
that turned careless ten year olds
to tender mothers,

a prince would scale the tower,
would stumble blinded
through the woods to find her.

Idols

I like to think of them just as they were.
Untested, they never fell from plinths,

a line of straight noses and perfect lips,
a frieze unspoilt by real proximity.

The blonde boy with the cowhorn handlebars
who sang like an angel and smoked Old Holborn,

the one with dark toffee eyes and silky hair
fluent in languages with a taste for jazz,

I wouldn't want to know them now, as men
in suits, with paunches, getting thin on top.

I didn't know them then, being out
of reach kept safe their immortality;

clothes and mannerisms, voices, all preserved,
I dust them off, return them to their shelf.

Tools

Once I used a chisel as a screwdriver.
My father ran his thumb
along the damaged edge,
silence worse than words.
All the hours of watching him,
I should have known the difference.

After he'd gone tools receded
to the backs of sheds, rusted amongst
other people's jumble, then I met you.
Your father was a tool maker.
You wouldn't confuse screwdriver and chisel.
Tools are easy in your hands.

You are making bookshelves
and my kitchen fills with echoes.
Settled by familiar rhythms,
I look back – the chisel's sharp again,
he's easing out a runnel from pale wood.
I'm at the table with my homework, watching.

Wishes

She is wearing pyjamas and her boat
is small as a walnut shell. She didn't
know the ocean was so big and night

so long. The pyjamas are pink with rabbits.
She managed all the buttons but forgot
her slippers and dark is sloshing round her feet.

She doesn't know if they're seeing
how far out she's got, shivering
with the night sea tossing her nut-shell boat,

if they are watching from inside those voices.
Fingers in her ears and eyes tight shut
she makes her wishes, as they do in books,

that the sea will be smooth in the morning,
that they will put on their everyday voices,
that there will be cornflakes and cats purring.

Looking into the Picture

I have been looking through this window
always – have traced the banisters' curve,
made mine the geraniums, the shadows.

Upstairs, the children are sleeping, sweet breathed,
hair in damp kisses on their skin,
limbs heavy, they are spread-eagled like stars.

Downstairs, the parents are full of silence,
the dazed puzzle of resentment as what
was woven is unravelling, their fingers

too clumsy to sort out the tangle. But
now there is another room further back
in the darkness and words are bruising

like stones, words are cutting like glass,
and a small ghost stands at the crack
of her door listening as the night breaks

apart. How did I not remember
when her room has always been there.

To My House

House, you are visited by sunlight.
It washes your rooms with morning
and as day closes the sinking sun
sheds low beams from Cornsay Colliery
painting your garden rosy.
Now late summer blousy, it wears
blue sea holly beside orange daisies,
purple loosestrife flecked with cabbage whites,
a last fling of colour and honey scents.
Crab apples are burnished beads;
vegetables harvested, only potatoes
are treasure waiting to be found.

Old house, your hums and clicks
have settled to a background music,
breath, heartbeat, pulse.
I have come to know your ways,
to love the shelter of your local brick
around my southern heart.
And as I sleep the ghosts of miners
pass up and down the stairs,
night shifts giving way to morning.
The shush of stockinged feet,
a floorboard's creak, slip
through the skin of my dreams.

Background Music

What were the paths that brought her to
this row of houses at the village edge?

The way it felt familiar was not ordinary.
Even before she'd filled them with her scent

the rooms said 'You are home', as if she could
drag in her bags of trouble and unpack them here.

Standing in the window watching
she is a child soothed by the oldest toy:

sheep wheel in a white tide, cows string out
in steady lines, calves are dancing dots.

Red combine labouring up the hill's flank,
the plough's new furrows in a cloud of gulls

uncover the rhythm she had forgotten,
the ground bass that she ceased to hear.

Between brick and concrete she lost
the pattern of pastures, copses, barns,

the shifts of landscape tamed by hedges,
villages creeping out into farmland.

The window frames an echo, gives her back
a hint of the wild at the edge of fields.

Deerness Valley

The farms were first, before the villages –
East Flass, Hare Holme, Hag House and Rowley,
they saw machines and men brought in
to disturb the landscape, saw terraced rows
spread out into communities.

The pit is local history now
kept under the caps of old bent men
who gather outside the post office.
They marvel at the village youngsters,
with their cars and college courses,
their eyes on the wider skies.

Sunday walkers startle deer and breathe
the windy air of ridge and valley view.
Woods give way to fields, fields to new estates.
High over the farms at night the lights of planes
track pathways out into the world and back.

South Derwentside

Satley Cowsley Quickburn Grange
Cornsay Quebec High Hermitage
Partridge Close Throstle Nest Farm
Whitehall Moss Buttsfield Burn
Salter's Gate New Ivesley
Greenacres Wilk's Hill Rowley
Greenland Standalone Steeley Burn
High Hedleyhope Stobbilee Farm
Broadmeadows Hag Wood Quick Burn
Rare Dean Stonefoot Hill Hare Holme Farm

Garden Birds

Tits in the hawthorn
turn blue-grey stone
frozen drops of nerve and down.

A wren rattling in the hedge
hop-drops from twig to twig,
her amplified rat-tat is small shot

cannot dislodge
death from his perch.

Only the eyes flicker.
       Claws grip the branch
in practice.

The blind corner swerve
the jet stream
send clouds of finches
dipping and turning.
Always the laggard
picked off
small soft fruit
plucked.

Winter's consolation
long-tailed tits
clustering on the peanuts
a neat meshing
of bold striped tails,
bodies pastel fluffballs,
       diminutive beaks
     see-see, see-see
thin notes
spilling.

Asylum

In flight from Scandinavian cold
a single fieldfare settles in my garden.
His mottled whites and browns
are perfect camouflage
among tussocks clotted with frozen snow.

He roots for windfalls,
holds bright beads of crab apples
in pincer beak, then swallows whole.
The native blackbird makes fierce sorties,
feathers funnelled into missile shape.
The thrush sits tight, blackbird retreats
to rattle in metallic bursts, staccato.

Fieldfares making this journey for centuries,
blackbirds holding the homeground,
skies crisscrossed by travellers,
more or less unwelcome –

In my garden's small kingdom I am god.
I decree there are windfalls enough
for a flock of foreign fieldfares.
I throw fat raisins to the angry blackbird.

Into Winter

I rake up leaves,
browns and yellows,
the odd flecks of red,
that damp smell of decay
beginning. Air has
a cold edge
an icy touch.
Old blooms turn crisp,
foliage brittle.

Birds rustle and hop
in the hawthorn,
keep me in view.
They are silent.
The robin's *tink tink*
quiet for once.
A vacuum –
breathless –
after the sparrowhawk.

On the bench
a greenfinch,
his wings a still ripple
of moss, of lime.
His dark eye stares,
head awkward, neck
broken in his flight from
death into the lying glass
of my window – a downy puff
marks the point of contact.

I would toss him up,
see his feathers stir again,
his wings flex and tilt.
But warmth is leaving him.
He is stiffening
into twig, husk.

December

Late sunrise and the stubble field is gold.
Day is just a moment held in night.
Black skeletons of trees stand stiff with cold.
Late sunrise and the stubble field is gold.
Summer is forgotten, its play of light.
Hold fast to what is hidden, what burns bright.
Late sunrise and the stubble field is gold.
Day is just a moment held in night.

January Meeting

Winter sun sharp focuses
frost glint on hawthorn,

wet green of first crop rows,
pale stubble, ploughed earth's purple.

Then light hits windscreens,
a line of vehicles waiting.

Men in caps, dark jackets, boots,
field glasses swinging loose.

I think of rare bird visitors
drawn to these wooded hills,

ask what they are looking at.
Hunt's out. And the morning blurs –

the panic chase, the blood, the men
who focus their binoculars like guns.

Clearing Ground

First deadhead the old blooms –
see how tenacious they are,
rattling with what's past.

Sweep out the dead leaves
ghosts of another season,
they muffle and cling.

Cut away the confusion,
the tangle of brittle twigs.
You must let in the light.

See how the blades bite.
Do not bruise the nerves,
nor touch the raw life.

Now picture the new blooms
opening soft throats
to the sun.

You must find the exact point
where the dead wood begins,
then cut it out.

It Was Not the Owl

It was not the owl that took her soul,
no silent wing beat to ruffle the dark,
no claws to clutch it, light as a mouse.
Yet night was robbed of all its secrets,
space between stars shrunk, the wild tamed.

It was not the hawk that took her soul,
no swerve of feathers freezing the garden,
no beak to tear it, plump as a fledgling.
Yet day was diluted, its colours pale,
bird notes were muffled, earth scents faint.

Better the feral cat on stealthy paws
stilling its flutter, ripping it open,
than her own neglect that left her soul
in an ordinary corner of everyday
to grow dull on a diet of dust.

Maisie Poems

Maisie had a head
full of whispers.
She clattered
through the days
covering the sibilance
with noise.
But it waited
on her pillow,
a voice that rustled,
shushing
her thinking
insinuating
hushed words
into her head.

Maisie hummed the words
to a single thread
wound it
round her fingers
rolled it
like a ball
into a forgotten
corner of her heart
to await the time
for the unravelling
of whispers
when the words
would shush
into another ear.

*

Maisie hides her left hand
like Napoleon
so you cannot see
it isn't there.

This is her best joke.

Who helped Maisie
cut her hands off?
Nobody.
That's why she has
one left. Right.

Maisie wonders
how much tenderness
she can dispense
with the one left.

*

Maisie knew a man
who threw
electric shavers at the wall
beside her.
They burst
in showers of springs and blades.
He had tempers big enough
to fill the stair well,
to rise
like ether
to their top flat.
They preceded him,
numbing floors and walls.
Maisie's head
learned to sing
so she could not hear him.

*

Maisie saw her life twice
fluttering high above her
a poor trapped bird.

The first time it bashed
against the hospital lights
of a birth.

The second time it flapped
against the blank ceiling
of a death.

She knew then
it would take some watching.

She learned to keep it away
from the lure of gas fires
the pull of high windows.

She tried to shelter it
in the twiggy nest of her heart.

Two Women

'While we sleep here, we are awake somewhere else,
so that every man is in fact two men.'
   Jorge Luis Borges

I think I saw her once.
Almost asleep, head on the pillow,
limbs curled warm, I seemed
to pause, almost to turn.

She was a faint outline
waiting for colour to flood in.
She was poised, standing.
Her back was turned.

She wore a cloak, a hood
or robe that might become
the purest cobalt, her wrists
circled with tiny beads and bells.

Her stature was familiar,
the landscape strange –
the earth a ruddy brown
with crops close sown.

Ahead of her were roofs –
a settlement – but whether
she was seeking refuge
or escape, I cannot know.

Even in stillness I felt
her urgency, as if her frozen
figure ached to be released.
I let her go. I slept.

Sister Veronique in the Valley of the Shadow

Her fingers miss the agate beads
her rosary from childhood
a grandmother's gift.

She knows it is a sin, that missing.

They were polished by prayer.
Her fingers knew their way
over the cool smoothness.

She knows she should not think of material things.

Rosary – rosarium – rose garden
a little girl, she used to think
they must be buds full of holiness.

She knows she should not dwell upon the past.

She wonders who it was who carved –
whose bones – why choose
to make such cruel beads.

You must think upon your own mortality, they said.

Her fingers fumble – eye socket, jaw.
She loses her way and the skulls grin –
her prayers are a puff of dust.

Encounter with Angels

If God is anywhere he should be here
in this cathedral with its feet in war.

In early morning quiet I light a candle
breathe in stillness, as if I belonged.

I know he isn't here but war makes me
long for miracles, a voice from the sky.

I would like a fiery descent into
this holy space, a cup full of suffering.

The pity of war whispers in every stone
but nobody seems to be listening.

A voice breaks into my meanderings.
God's mouthpiece is a woman in black robes.

I say I am thinking about the war.
She says all will be clear to us in time.

She asks me what else we can do with evil.
The gates of my heart clang shut.

It was the tumbling angels that opened them,
etched figures in the wall of glass, pure motion.

It was the windows' blaze of colour, the cross
of nails, the imagery of thread and stone.

Epstein knew what to do with evil.
He made a thickset devil whose chains

threaten to loose him, and a sinewy saint
whose wings give him the edge, just about.

The struggle is there in muscle and tendon,
wings against horns, it bursts from the bronze.

Coventry 2003

Misericords

Though brothers they are not my brothers.
They are not even proper men, my father
says, and dares to carve them lustful pigs
to shame them. I am his apprentice.
I am learning how to see what lies
within the dark oak – it may be trees,
or Jonah and his whale – how to find
the tool whose edge will free them, hidden
creatures that wait within the wood.

Old Brother Anselm has a good heart.
He breaks a hunk of new baked bread for me.
For him I found a dainty unicorn.
But Brother Hugh is harsh. He cuffed my ear
because I dipped my fingers in the honey.
His hand was heavy like a proper man's.
For him to rest his arse on I have found
a hedgepig with the sharpest spines.

French Polish

I haunt the soirée. They do not see me.
Words gather to a single buzz, waver
when a squawk, a shriek, a cackle breaks,
then settle back to buzz. I watch the man's
fat fingers skim the table's polished skin.

I think of it as mine. I hear him say
I have a chap called Jean who travels
for me – Thailand, India – I've never been.
A girl's hand now upon the table's shine,
I flinch as she puts a wine glass down.

Imagine the forest, the steamy heat,
how Jean was paying us to scale the trunks,
shinning up, half naked, with a blade
to chip it off, a pouch to keep it safe.
Too easy then to lose a footing,

as I lost mine. If she could hear me
I would whisper like a breeze into her ear,
What you are touching when you touch this sheen
are the resin traces of a thousand
beetles, collected by dead boys like me.

No Place

With your finger on the machine
they know who you are.
Only your print is truthful.
Hold out your arms.
You must bring in nothing.
Someone accompanies you
with rattling chain and keys
to open each metal gate.

They hold dogs on a tight leash.
When they are moving the men
you must be locked inside.
Bright lights shine on tables,
paints, books, guitars, shine
on men sitting, talking
or silent, head in hands.
There are no windows.

Once I was squeezed between
rock ceiling and rock floor,
dragging along like a lizard,
making for light and air,
limbs petrifying. It is like that.
Something has been sucked out
of the air, something is missing.
Blood slows. You could not run.

Her Grandmother's Soup

Before she left she put on the stiff apron
to fetch the vegetables one last time.

The soil was too hard that day to yield more.
She scrubbed and sliced, hands red from the juice.

She set the pan to bubble, waited to add
salt and cream before she struck the bell.

She filled her mother's bowl to the brim
with her grandmother's soup. She would not eat.

*

Here feels to her already like heaven.
The voices lift her into clear blue.

Order and peace, they say, order and peace.
They offer her a draught of melted snow.

Her feet are new born on the cloister tiles.
She left home behind in her boot treads.

Miss Hartley's Deerhounds

So that they might lope to the moment of exhaustion and know it,
Miss Hartley put no collars on her deerhounds before twelve
months.

Contained in suit and brogues, with tight-bunned hair she let them
stretch their long legs, feel the muscles work in abdomen and
haunch.

She liked the height of deerhounds, the way she could slip the
collars on
without the need to bend, the way their shaggy heads were just hip
level.

Miss Hartley's deerhounds speed across moor and stream, burrs
and thistles
catching in their coats, they are grey wraiths of legend in their silent
passing.

Along the sand they bound, dipping and leaping, shrouds of sea
mist drifting.
Necks stretched, ears blown back, they are slate and pewter spun
into foam.

As they near the moment how their rough coats shine, turn pearl,
turn silver
as they curl and tremble, arch their backs like breakers, melt away,
like spray.

Reunion

He asks if she remembers.
She cannot tell.
Her hands twist in her lap.
Later she will say.

He thinks how she was sunshine,
once a gazelle.
In dreams his eyes are bright.
Now she dare not look.

She asks what he remembers.
He cannot say.
Twist of the heart again,
years falling away.

Her pulse is a broken tune,
His breath a sigh.
Love is an awkward ghost
returning too soon.

Ex-lovers

They are guests at the end of an evening
who cannot find their hats, their gloves;
who are sure they left a coat upstairs,
and must just say this final thing.
They materialise in quiet moments
causing a pang, a blush, a flash of rage,
or bluff their way into dreams
where they sit on chairs and turn eloquent
as if they had a right to be there.
They are boxes of secrets best kept shut.
They have albums full of evidence,
letters that prove who they were.
They hover at the edges, whispering
Remember this. Remember what you said.

Grandmother's Portrait, 1890

sit still   scarcely breathe
slow blink   camera's eye
best dress   black dress

(oh remember sprigged muslin
pastel silks and ribbons)

stiff pleats   high neck
close sleeves   neat cuffs
skirt rustles   skirt swishes

(old lady   it whispers)

hair smooth   pulled back
central parting   white line
tight knot   sharp pins

(oh ringlets brushing skin
loose curls bouncing)

sit still   no smile
face stiff   eyes stern
hands rest   heart thuds

(grandmother's portrait
scarcely breathe)

Lily

She does not remember swallowing
the fish hook but it is fixed
in the tissue at the back of her throat.

It has slipped home like the fasteners
on her bodice and her fingers were too thick
to reach it – how she gagged and choked.

At first she didn't know there was a line
attached – a line so fine she cannot
see it, knows it only by the tug

when she laughs or when she cries out loud.
So now she must speak only soft and low.
If she forgets, if she lets excitement

bubble up, or anger, how it snags,
how it tears, until she moans
without moving her mouth or her throat.

Lily is quiet-spoken, they say,
so modest and still – a real lady.
They do not see she is a fish gasping.

Looking for Shells

She dresses in black silk.
It slips and whispers.

The light is brackish –
an underwater realm.

She sits in the oak rocker.
The past floats by in shoals.

She has only to reach out
to catch a bright sliver

to turn it over and over
until it lives in her hand.

There is the bathing hut,
the bank of wet shingle.

She is sifting the pebbles
looking for shells.

My Grandmother Waiting

i.m. John Jeans 1899–1918, Charlotte Jeans 1874–1922

After more than a year of silence the letter came
with its one plain story in the voice of authority;

a form letter, the spaces filled in with the name
of her boy, his rank, his regiment, his number.

She did what she must – put his photo in the paper,
answered the letters that offered new chapters of a story –

he was wounded, captured, in a camp in Poland, there was
a photo, he was there – see the Devonshire cap badge.

Each was a possible plot, an easing of the dread.
Letters crisscrossed the country – mothers, sweethearts, sisters

keeping their boys alive a little longer, seeing their likenesses
in the photos that were not like them, in the accounts that did
                                                              not fit.

She spun out the stories, made slight chances certainties
for weeks, for months, for years. If the day ever came

when all the stories faded, their words washed away leaving
only blank pages – it was the day her life ended.

Playing Grandmother

Other grandmas wore print aprons,
carried shopping in proper baskets.
Mine inhabited stories of war –

my father's mother, Charlotte, slipping
from grief to death when her elder son
failed to come back from the trenches;

Lily dying in 1943, my mother
travelling north with a baby
to show her, on trains packed with troops.

My grandmas faded in darkened rooms
before they could take on the role.
Even my mother managed only months.

Now it's my turn. I know the lines
but have no costume – I'm trying
to find my feet on unsteady ground.

I need to negotiate time's
strange collapses – a stance or smile
that hurtles me backwards – this baby

turns into her father on my knee;
this toddler arranges pebbles
in a perfect curve, as his father did.

Time traveller grandma, I'm back
where nursery cosiness gives way
to sudden drops of fear,

where small hands' hot grip is an anchor,
where love comes sharp as a stitch.

Tug

My heart is beating
with a small piece missing.

The tenderness started
before you were here.

Then when they announced you
I felt the pull,

a small piece parting
to settle with you.

You will not see it,
may sense it sometimes

a cocoon of sunshine
light as air.

My heart is learning
its new raw edges,

the sudden tug of
your long distance line.

Baby Monitor

Night has become a box of sounds.
I must not stop listening
for the hush, hush of butterfly breath.
Night noises squeeze in,
a car's tin rattle, a startled squawk,
far off voices, a dog's one bark.
Bricks shift, house clicks and creaks.

I am listening hard and silence is rushing
between the sounds as if it might
sweep away the shush of a stirring limb,
the murmur as lips part, might wash
over that miniscule change in the breath's
flutter, that falter in the rhythm
that would have me out of bed, in time.

Unsafe Territory

Back in the unsafe territory
I hold small hands, decipher wants,
give my whole day's concentration,
slowing my pace to their time.

Water is deep, cars speed, dogs bite.
Though older I've no spells or charms.
Worry settles on the heart.
When did I forget this squeezing,

this nocturnal weight pressing down?
I tell myself how they are loved,
how they have sturdy bodies,
minds that brim with schemes and fancy.

But worry has found out the heart's
weak point, the lurching fear. Knowing
my sons as fathers holds this pain –
I may not see these children grown.

At Tentsmuir

for Roberta

Late summer sunshine is slipping in and out
of cloud, the air salt-washed and shining,
only the pine trees are holding darkness.
Freed from clothes the small boy hesitates,
watches wind crease the pool's surface,
his sturdy body stippling with cold.
Better to dress again, to run, to draw
fierce monsters in the sand, then watch the tide
creep up to swallow pool and monsters.

I hold this baby – I hardly know him yet.
It suits him looking outwards, back
against my belly. I feel the tremor
as he kicks and murmurs at the sea,
blowing his excitement out in bubbles.
This is the heart of it – sons bringing wives
to be new daughters, children to share in.
Life allowing me a rare revisit
to the firstness of everything.

Guests

Awe at the first arrival,
they turned up with wet plastered hair
faces flattened by travel,

journey's end the heart centre.
They stayed, settled in
grew familiar, departed.

Years of living together
concentrate down to a weekend visit
lit by anticipation,

the most honoured guests
for whom dishes, towels, sheets
are embellished with love.

Visit over
a phone call sets them
safe in their grown up lives.

Silence has changed into
absence of voices,
the small house too spacious,

washing and folding,
to pack love away again
hard to find room on the shelf.

Lendings

More often now, sitting quiet
at the table reading or
standing at the window,
a door opens a crack then shuts,

as if the skin of the day splits,
or night blinks a dark eye.
There is a stop to time's ticking.
Fear freezes my outbreath out.

I almost glimpse, but catch only
the edges of a passing
where darkness shades into
the coldest shadow, with no sun.

Against the silence of alone
I gather to me what life lends,
the best loved voices, birdsong,
children laughing in the garden.

No Fairy Story

for D.H.J 1907–1975

She didn't need a magic mirror.
Her presence was so strong in me
that even when she wasn't there
I knew she might be. Too honest to lie to,
she was a stream too clear to muddy.

The one time that I really needed her
she came like Demeter across the miles,
straight from the top step of the ladder
not waiting to brush the distemper
from her hair. She came with her belief,
lighting small tapers in the deepest dark.

Now she would be a hundred – thinking
conjures her back across the gulf.
She's covering the years in seven-league
strides, scattering all the stars in her wake.

Acknowledgements

Some of these poems were first published in *Artemis, Diamond Twig* website, *Gate gate, Other Poetry, Sand, 2nd Light*; in Neil Astley (ed.) *Being Alive* (Bloodaxe Books, 2004), Bob Beagrie and Andy Willoughby (eds), *The Wilds* (Ek Zuban, 2007). 'Deerness Valley' was commissioned by Culture North East.

Cynthia Fuller wishes to thank Tess Spencer for permission to use her painting 'Esh Winning' as the front cover image for this book.